L.H.

Hard-Work Wheels

by **Debora Pearson**
illustrations by **Chum McLeod**

Annick Press Ltd.
Toronto • New York • Vancouver

For my son, Benjamin
—D.P.

Annick Press Ltd.

We acknowledge the support of the Canada Council for the Arts, the Ontario Arts Council, and the Government of Canada through the Book Publishing Industry Development Program (BPIDP) for our publishing activities.

The Publisher gratefully acknowledges the permission to use the registered trademark, ZAMBONI, as well as an image of the Zamboni Ice Resurfacer in this publication.

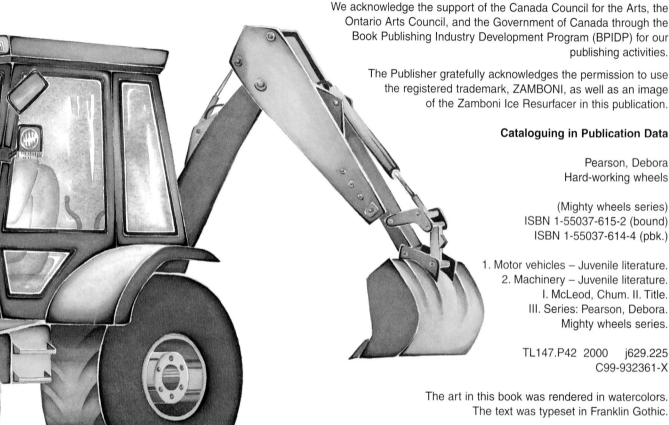

Cataloguing in Publication Data

Pearson, Debora
Hard-working wheels

(Mighty wheels series)
ISBN 1-55037-615-2 (bound)
ISBN 1-55037-614-4 (pbk.)

1. Motor vehicles – Juvenile literature.
2. Machinery – Juvenile literature.
I. McLeod, Chum. II. Title.
III. Series: Pearson, Debora.
Mighty wheels series.

TL147.P42 2000   j629.225
C99-932361-X

The art in this book was rendered in watercolors.
The text was typeset in Franklin Gothic.

Distributed in Canada by:
Firefly Books Ltd.
3680 Victoria Park Avenue
Willowdale, ON
M2H 3K1

Published in the U.S.A. by Annick Press (U.S.) Ltd.
Distributed in the U.S.A. by:
Firefly Books (U.S.) Inc.
P.O. Box 1338
Ellicott Station
Buffalo, NY 14205

Printed and bound in Canada by Friesens, Altona, Manitoba.

A backhoe scoops up a load of dirt … A fire truck shoots by on its way to a blaze … For a toddler or preschooler, these aren't just machines at work. They're creatures on wheels – immense, noisy, active and, above all, amazing!

Looking at motor vehicles and talking about them are some of the simplest forms of entertainment around. They're also great ways to share basic ideas and concepts with young children. As you make your way through this book you can talk about what's fast and what's slow, what's noisy and what's quiet, what's up close and what's far away. Together you can imagine what you might choose from the snack truck and make up your own siren sounds as you look at the ladder truck and ambulance. It's all part of the best show on the road, and it's waiting for you inside *Hard-Working Wheels.*

What's that rumble? What's that roar?
Hard-working wheels are on the go.

A tractor drags a heavy plow that combs the lumpy earth. Soon seeds will be planted there.

**Load up some kids, load up some books,
load up some lunches, and add lots of noise.**

**Then trek to school and let out the load –
that's what a school bus does each day.**

A cherry picker st-r-r-r-r-etches
out its long steel arm. It reaches
for the power lines that need to
be repaired.

Getting louder . . . louder . . . LOUD!
A ladder truck flashes by, off to fight
a fire. Soon its ladder will unfold to
reach the highest flames.

A spurting, squirting pumper truck hoses down the blaze. Fierce hot flames fizzle out when they're soaked with water.

A snack truck lugs a load of food to the construction site. Sip here, slurp here. Gobble up some grub here.

A bulldozer crawls over rubble, shoving rocks and smoothing dirt.

A busy backhoe has a seat that can twirl all the way around. The driver faces forward to lift the wide loader.

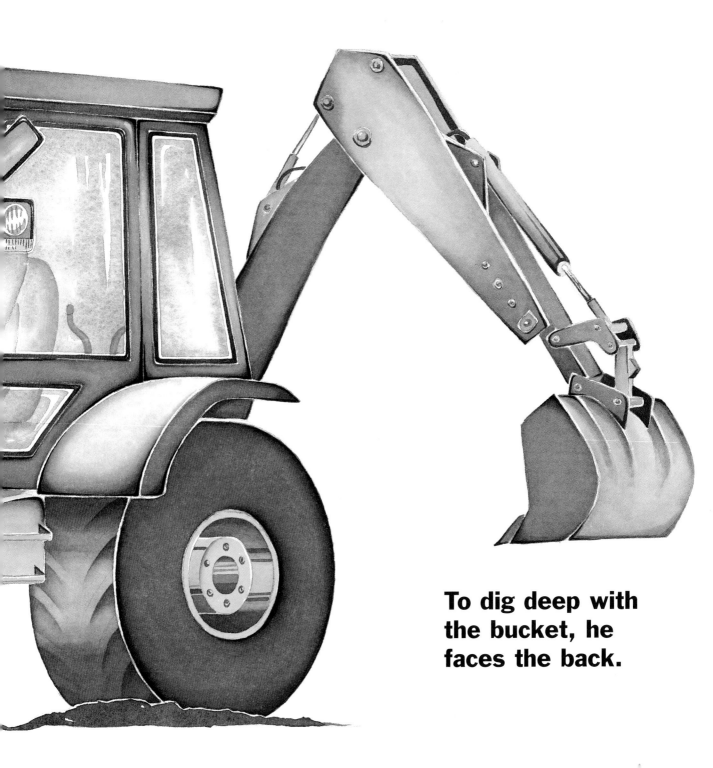

To dig deep with the bucket, he faces the back.

**Want to look at a funny book? A scary book?
A sleepy bedtime storybook?**

Then step into the bookmobile. It carries a little library to people in many places.

An ambulance screams to the scene
when people need help in a hurry.

Shhhhh! A police car is out on patrol.
Turn off the siren, go s-l-o-w.

A street cleaner creeps over the street, spinning its dusty brushes. It eats up dirt and leaves behind a clean, wet trail of water.

A Zamboni rolls over the rink, scraping up ice chips and gulping them down. It washes the rink and leaves behind smooth new ice on top.

**Moving people, clearing snow . . .
hard-working wheels always help out.**